DEAR BROTHER

by Frank Asch / Vladimir Vagin

SCHOLASTIC
HARDCOVER

SCHOLASTIC INC.

New York

Library of Congress Cataloging-in-Publication Data

Asch, Frank.
Dear brother / by Frank Asch, Vladimir Vagin.
p.   cm.
Summary: Joey and Marvin stay up all night reading a collection
of funny letters that they found in the attic.
ISBN 0-590-43107-2
[1. Brothers – Fiction.   2. Letters – Fiction.   3. Country life—
Fiction.   4. City and town life – Fiction] .   I. Vagin, Vladimir
Vasil'evich. 1937 –   . II. Title.
PZ7.A778De   1991
[E]–dc20   90-45258
                                                                 CIP
                                                                 AC

12 11 10 9 8 7 6 5 4 3 2 1   2 3 4 5 6 7/9
Printed in the U.S.A.   36

First Scholastic printing, March 1992

Designed by Frank Asch, Claire Counihan,
and Vladimir Vagin

This artwork was painted with
dyes, gouache, and
watercolor.

To Patricia Winpenny

ONE DAY Joey and Marvin were helping their mother
clean out the attic.

"You're not going to throw out my sled, are you?" asked Joey.

"Of course not, cheesebrain!" said Marvin. "We're just
getting rid of the old stuff."

"What about this old stack of letters?"

"I wish we could save everything, Joey," said his mother.

"But we've got to make some space up here for new things."

Joey looked at one of the letters and noticed that
it was illustrated with interesting pictures.

"Can I keep them?"

"Only if you don't store them up here," said his mother.

When Joey, Marvin, and their mother were finished, they hauled everything they wanted to throw away down to the street for the garbage mouse to pick up in the morning.

After dinner Joey went upstairs and untied the stack
of old letters.

"Well, pack rat," said Marvin, "what are you going
to do with those dusty old letters?"

"Read them," said Joey, and he opened the first letter.

Dear Brother Timothy,

At last I have a few moments to write. Since waving good-bye to you all from the train I've had quite an adventure. Remember how Poppa told me to hide all my money inside my hat? Well, that's just what I did. But when the train sped past a circus parade I stuck my head out the window to catch a glimpse of the show. All of a sudden a big gust of wind took hold of my hat and sent it flying like a barn swallow!

When I arrived in the city I had no money. I couldn't even buy a tiny slice of cheese. Renting a room was out of the question. I was cold and hungry. For hours I did nothing but wander the streets. That night I was forced to sleep under a bridge. But the next morning I looked up and saw **my hat** floating down the river!

With a long stick I fished it out and found all my money tucked safely under the brim.

What a relief!

The first thing I did was buy myself some cheese. Then I rented a room. Tomorrow I will go and look for a job. So please tell Momma and Poppa that I am doing fine in the big city and all is well with me.

Love, Brother Henry

P.S. Now that I have a place to live you can come and visit anytime.

"I wonder who Henry was?" said Joey when he finished reading the letter.

"Don't you know anything?" said Marvin. "Henry was our great-great-granduncle."

"I'm pretty sure one of those pictures out there is his,"
said Marvin.

Joey thought the old portraits looked sad in the moonlight.

Slowly he opened another letter.

DEAR BROTHER HENRY,

MOMMA AND POPPA SAID TO SAY HELLO AND TELL YOU HOW MUCH THEY MISS YOU TOO. YESTERDAY I FORGOT YOU WERE GONE AND SET A PLACE FOR YOU AT THE DINNER TABLE. MOMMA MADE CHEESE SOUP JUST THE WAY YOU LIKE IT.

I HAVEN'T HAD ANY ADVENTURES LIKE THE ONE YOU DESCRIBE IN YOUR LETTER. BUT THIS MORNING POPPA HITCHED UP THE NEW HORSE AND SHOWED ME HOW TO PLOW. I DID ALL RIGHT UNTIL I SAID "GO!" INSTEAD OF "WHOA!"

AND DUG UP MOMMA'S FAVORITE FLOWER BED.

WHILE POPPA FINISHED THE PLOWING I WENT DOWN TO OUR SECRET FISHING HOLE AND CAUGHT A BIG FISH. I HAD FUN BUT IT WOULD HAVE BEEN EVEN MORE FUN IF YOU HAD BEEN THERE. I WAS GOING TO DRAW A PICTURE OF THE FISH TO SEND TO YOU, BUT ONE OF THE BARN CATS ATE IT WHILE I WENT TO FETCH MY PEN AND INK.

SO HERE'S A PICTURE OF THE BONES:

HENRY, I KNOW HOW MUCH YOU'VE ALWAYS DREAMED OF LIVING IN THE CITY. BUT IF THINGS AREN'T GOING WELL PLEASE DON'T FEEL LIKE YOU HAVE TO PRETEND OTHERWISE.

I HAVEN'T TOUCHED A THING IN YOUR OLD ROOM

YOUR BED IS MADE AND READY TO SLEEP IN WHENEVER YOU WANT **TO COME HOME.**

LOVE,
BROTHER Timothy

P. S. NO NEED FOR ME TO VISIT AS I EXPECT YOU'LL BE HOME REAL SOON.

When Joey was finished reading he went to
the window.

"I bet the one in the white hat is Great-great-
granduncle Henry," he said, "and the one in the straw
hat is Great-great-granduncle Timothy."

"No kidding, Sherlock!" said Marvin.

"It's getting late," said Mother. "Better turn out the lights and go to bed."

"I guess we'll read the rest of the letters tomorrow," said Joey.

"That's what a goody-goody would do," said Marvin.

And he covered their bunk bed with blankets.

"But Mom said—" began Joey.

"She said 'go to bed,'" said Marvin as he turned
on his flashlight. "She didn't say 'go to sleep.'"

Dear Brother Timothy,

Good news! I got a job. It's just sewing buttons in a small tailor shop. But it's a beginning. Mr. Pinhead, the owner of the shop, says I have good paws. Maybe someday

I'll be a real tailor!

I also sweep the floor and wait on customers, and sometimes I wear an advertisement sign and walk through the streets.

It made me homesick to hear of Momma's cheese soup. But I am learning to cook for myself. Yesterday I put a pot of rice on the stove to boil and leaned out my window to watch what was going on in the street.

After a while I saw a fire truck pull up. Everyone was so excited. "Look at all the smoke!" they cried. Then I turned around and saw that the smoke was coming from my pot of rice!

Timothy, I miss you so much. But I love my new life in the city.

For me it is a dream come true. I doubt that I'll be coming home to visit until holiday time. So with my first paycheck I bought a ticket for you to visit. I'm also sending some postcards for Poppa and a new hat for Momma.

Love, Brother *Henry*

DEAR BROTHER HENRY,

MOMMA AND POPPA SEND THEIR LOVE. POPPA SAID TO TELL YOU THANKS FOR THE POSTCARDS. AND MOMMA LIKED THE PRETTY CITY HAT YOU SENT HER.

POPPA HUNG THE POSTCARDS IN THE BARN FOR THE CHICKENS TO LOOK AT WHILE THEY LAY

E G G S,

AND MOMMA WENT TO CHURCH

TWICE

LAST SUNDAY

SO EVERYONE IN TOWN COULD GET A CHANCE TO SEE

HER PRETTY NEW HAT.

HENRY, AFTER READING YOUR LAST LETTER I'M MORE CONVINCED THAN EVER THAT YOU OUGHT TO COME HOME AS SOON AS POSSIBLE. THE CITY SEEMS TO HAVE DULLED YOUR BRAIN. WALKING THROUGH THE STREET DISGUISED AS A BOOK DOES NOT SEEM LIKE A DECENT WAY FOR A MOUSE TO EARN A LIVING! I ALSO fEAR THAT

YOUR LIFE IS IN DANGER

IF YOU CONTINUE TO EXPERIMENT WITH COOKING. I DON'T KNOW WHAT IT IS YOU LIKE ABOUT THE BIG CITY BUT I'M SURE YOU'LL BE HAPPIER IN THE COUNTRY WHERE YOU BELONG.

LOVE,
BROTHER Timothy

P. S. I'M SENDING BACK YOUR TICKET SO YOU CAN USE IT YOURSELF TO COME HOME.

ONE TICKET
from country to city
ONE FARE

Dear Brother Timothy,

City life has not dulled my brain. Indeed, if anyone's brain has been dulled *it's yours!*

For your information I do not make my living by disguising myself as a book. And anyone can burn a pot of rice whether they live in the city or the country!

I know city life has its problems. There're too many pickpockets, and not enough green grass and blue skies. But the country isn't perfect either. And it just so happens that I don't like plowing fields, stacking hay, fixing fences and chasing **stray cows**.

I don't like the mud and mosquitos and getting up in the middle of the night **to nurse a sick pig!**

Though I was born in the country, I'm a city mouse at heart. Maybe city life isn't really any better than country life. But it's better for me!

Timothy, you will always be my brother. But sometimes I fear that unless you make an effort to understand and accept me the way I am, we may drift apart and cease to be friends.

Love,
Brother Henry

Joey and Marvin read letter after letter
after letter until Marvin suddenly got out of bed.
"Where are you going?" asked Joey.
"Outside to get those portraits," said Marvin.
"But it's dark outside!" said Joey.
"I'm no scaredy-mouse!" said Marvin.

When he came back, Marvin put the two portraits
at the foot of the bunk bed.

Then he climbed in and they read on into the night.

DEAR BROTHER HENRY,

WHEN I FIRST READ YOUR LETTER I DIDN'T EVEN FEEL LIKE WRITING BACK, BUT THEN SOMETHING HAPPENED THAT MADE ME CHANGE MY MIND. REMEMBER THE DAY WE SAT UNDER THE OLD APPLE TREE AND PROMISED NEVER TO GROW UP AND FALL IN LOVE? WELL,

NEVER   NEVER

I'M AFRAID THE WORST ~~HAS~~ HAS HAPPENED!

LAST SATURDAY NIGHT I WENT TO THE CHERRY BLOSSOM FESTIVAL AND DANCED EVERY DANCE WITH MOLLY FLOWER. (ONLY STEPPED ON HER TAIL TWICE.)

AFTERWARDS,

I GAVE MOLLY A RIDE HOME IN THE OLD BUGGY. AND WHEN WE SAID GOOD NIGHT, WE KISSED IN THE MOONLIGHT. I WAS SO HAPPY ON THE WAY HOME I JUMPED OUT OF THE BUGGY AND DID A HEADSTAND IN THE BROOK.

YES, I'M IN LOVE

HENRY, I HOPE YOU FORGIVE ME FOR BREAKING MY PROMISE AND THE FOOLISH THINGS I SAID IN MY LAST FEW LETTERS. IF YOU LOVE THE CITY THEN THAT'S WHERE YOU BELONG. AND I WILL NEVER AGAIN TRY TO CHANGE YOUR MIND.

LOVE,
BROTHER Timothy

Dear Brother Timothy,

Your last letter made my whiskers tingle with delight. And the most wonderful thing of all is that **I, too, have fallen in love!**

Her name is Sara and I met her in a most unusual way.

Ever since Mr. Pinhead showed me how to mend with needle and thread, I've been working extra hours past closing time. Last night after locking up the shop I was so tired, instead of walking home I decided to take a bus.

My mind was weary from so many long hours of work. When I noticed that the mouse standing next to me at the bus stop had a tear in her jacket, I absentmindedly took out my needle and thread and began to mend it.

Unfortunately, the mouse thought I was trying to pick her pocket and began to holler for the police. When they arrived I was so embarrassed. The more I tried to explain, the more my explanation sounded like a made-up story. It was really quite a scene.

The next thing I knew I was behind bars! **WHAT A DISGRACE!** Luckily when the mouse returned home she found my needle in her coat. At once she hurried to the police station and convinced them that I was innocent.

And that's how I met my future wife. Yes, Timothy, Sara and I plan to be married in the fall! I do hope you and Molly can come to the wedding. I've already begun work on my wedding suit. Unfortunately, as you can see, it's a little too large.

Love,
Brother Henry

P.S. You sent back the ticket but I'd still like to send you a present. Any suggestions?

DEAR BROTHER HENRY,

CONGRATULATIONS! WHAT MARVELOUS NEWS! AND WONDER OF WONDERS I TOO HAVE SOME MARVELOUS NEWS.

MOLLY AND I ARE ALSO PLANNING TO BE MARRIED IN THE FALL! WHEN MOMMA AND POPPA HEARD THE NEWS, POPPA BROKE OUT HIS FIDDLE AND MOMMA STARTED DANCING ON THE KITCHEN TABLE!

OF COURSE THEY WANT US TO HAVE A DOUBLE WEDDING. I DON'T KNOW HOW YOU AND SARA FEEL ABOUT IT, BUT MOLLY AND I THINK IT'S A GREAT IDEA. MOMMA WANTS TO HAVE THE CEREMONY IN THE CITY AND THEN INVITE EVERYONE OUT TO THE COUNTRY FOR THE RECEPTION! SO LET ME KNOW WHAT YOU THINK. AND OH YES, BEFORE I FORGET, MOLLY SAID TO TELL SARA THAT SHE FAVORS THIS SHADE OF PINK FOR THE COLOR OF THE BRIDESMAIDS' DRESSES BUT ANY COLOR SARA LIKES WOULD BE JUST FINE.

LOVE,
BROTHER *Timothy*

P.S. ABOUT THAT SUIT. IT DEFINITELY LOOKS TOO LARGE FOR YOU, BUT I THINK IT MIGHT FIT ME JUST FINE. WHY DON'T YOU SEND IT TO ME AND I'LL TRY IT ON. IT CERTAINLY WOULD BE AN HONOR TO BE MARRIED IN A SUIT SEWN BY MY

VERY OWN BROTHER!

Joey and Marvin read many letters that night.
They read about Henry's life in the city with Sara
and Timothy's life in the country with Molly.

Dear Brother Timothy,

Sorry I haven't written for a while but Sara and I have been quite busy **moving into our new apartment**. It certainly has been a chore. When our new piano was

delivered, the three **strong moving mice** we hired to carry it up the stairs couldn't even lift it. I tried to help but it was still **too heavy**, and no one else on the street would stop to lend a paw. When Sara said, "Let me help," the three big moving mice just laughed. "Step aside!" said Sara and she proudly sat down at the piano and began to play. Oh my! What music she coaxed out of those piano keys. It was heavenly! First one mouse, then another and another gathered around to listen. When she was finished, several of those mice volunteered to help carry the piano up the stairs. Then the three big moving mice lifted my Sara onto their shoulders and **everyone cheered! It was quite a moment.** That's all for now.

Love,
Brother Henry

P.S. I'm sending you a photograph from the wedding. You have to admit Poppa certainly was the life of the party. I'll never forget how silly he looked swinging from the chandelier like a monkey. Too bad the chandelier broke—.

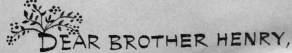

DEAR BROTHER HENRY,

THIS AFTERNOON I HAD QUITE AN ADVENTURE. IT STARTED WHEN I WENT OUT TO THE FOREST TO CHOP SOME EXTRA FIREWOOD. **I WAS CUTTING DOWN A LARGE ELM** WHEN MY AX **SLIPPED** AND **I FELL** TO THE GROUND. BEFORE I COULD GET UP **THE ELM FELL ON TOP OF ME! I CALLED OUT FOR HELP BUT NO ONE CAME.**

PINNED UNDER THAT TREE I HAD LOTS OF TIME TO THINK. I REMEMBERED MANY AMUSING EVENTS FROM THE PAST LIKE THE TIME WE DRESSED ALL OF POPPA'S COWS IN MOMMA'S DRESSES, AND THE DAY WE TOOK A SNAKE TO SCHOOL. THEN **A HUGE BEAR CAME OUT** OF THE FOREST.

IT WAS THE BIGGEST MEANEST BEAR I EVER SAW. I REALLY THOUGHT HE WAS GOING TO EAT ME FOR LUNCH. BUT THE BEAR WAS ONLY INTERESTED IN SOME RED BERRIES GROWING UNDERNEATH THE ELM TREE. WHEN HE MOVED THE ELM TO GET AT THE BERRIES **I WAS ABLE TO FREE MYSELF!** I FELT SO LUCKY JUST TO BE ALIVE. AS SOON AS I RETURNED HOME I SAT DOWN AND WROTE YOU THIS LETTER.

LOVE, BROTHER *Timothy*

P.S. THIS YEAR AT THE COUNTY FAIR POPPA WON THE FIDDLING CONTEST FOR THE **THIRD** STRAIGHT YEAR IN A ROW AND MOLLY USED MOMMA'S RECIPE FOR STRAWBERRY JAM AND WON A BLUE RIBBON. BUT THE MOST AMAZING THING WAS **THE FIRST PRIZE I GOT FOR MY CARROT.** IT REALLY WAS **HUGE!** I NOTICED THAT THE SEED LOOKED DIFFERENT WHEN I PLANTED IT BUT I NEVER EXPECTED SUCH RESULTS. MOLLY THINKS THE SEED CAME FROM ANOTHER WORLD, WHERE MICE ARE NO BIGGER THAN MITTENS. **WHAT A STRANGE IDEA!**

They read all night long until they came
to the last letter.

Dear Brother Timothy,

I hope you can read my handwriting because it's gotten very shaky of late.

My eyesight isn't what it used to be either. Last night Sara and I got dressed up to go to the opera but ended up at the circus instead. Sara kept telling me we made a mistake but I wouldn't believe her until I heard **the lions roar.**

All these years I've enjoyed my life as a city mouse but more and more I keep thinking about those early years when I lived in the country. I remember the smell of lilac in the spring and those lazy summer days when we **would go fishing.** So I've been thinking of coming out to visit for one last time. Sara would like to come too. Maybe you and I can go fishing like we used to when we were young. Then we could pick some cherries and help Molly and Sara bake a cherry pie.

Love, Brother *Henry*

P. S. When I come I'm going to bring all the letters you've written me over the years. Yes, I've saved every one as I know you've saved all of mine. I think we ought to keep them together just in case someone might want to **read them some day.**

"I wish there were more letters to read,"
said Joey. "I wonder why they stopped writing?"

"Maybe they just got too old to write anymore,"
said Marvin as he wrapped up the letters and put
them in a safe place. "Or maybe Henry moved back to
the country so they didn't have to write anymore."

"I'm so tired," said Joey.

"Me too," said Marvin, "but I'm sure glad
you saved those letters."

"Good night, Marvin,"
said Joey with a sleepy smile.
And Marvin smiled back.
"Good night, dear brother."